STARS

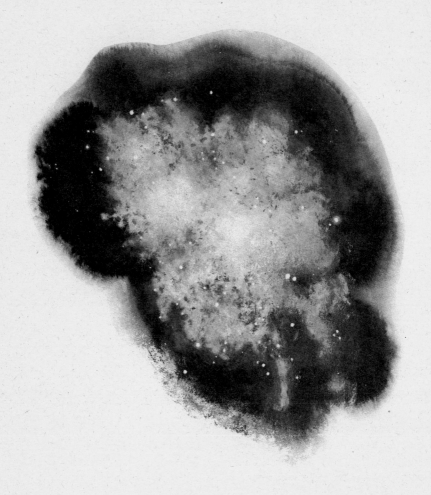

Troll Associates

STARS

by Louis Sabin

Illustrated by Andres Acosta

Troll Associates

Library of Congress Cataloging in Publication Data

Sabin, Louis.
   Stars.

   Summary: Explains the composition of stars, and the
nature of constellations and galaxies.
    1. Stars—Juvenile literature. [1. Stars] I. Acosta,
Andres, ill. II. Title.
QB801.7.S23   1985   523.8   84-2605
ISBN 0-8167-0152-0 (lib. bdg.)
ISBN 0-8167-0153-9 (pbk.)

There is nothing more beautiful than a sky full of stars on a clear, clear night. The stars look like diamonds glittering on a black velvet cloth.

But stars are not really diamonds. They are gigantic balls of gas that burn all the time. And like the flames of burning candles, the stars give off light and heat. We can see the light of the stars when we look at the night sky. But we cannot feel the heat they

give off, because the stars are so far away.

We do feel the heat from one star. That is our sun, the star closest to Earth. The sun is many millions of miles from our planet, but because all the other stars are so much farther away, their heat does not affect us.

How big is the sun compared to other stars? Dwarf stars are much smaller than our sun. But giant stars are much larger. And supergiants—the biggest stars—are larger still.

Picture a beach ball and a grain of sand. The beach ball stands for one of the largest stars, and the grain of sand stands for our sun. That's quite a difference! But most stars are about the same size as our sun. They are called medium-sized stars.

The sun is so close to Earth that light from the sun takes just eight minutes to reach us. Light from the next closest star, named Proxima Centauri, takes about four years to reach us. So we say that Proxima Centauri is four light years from the Earth.

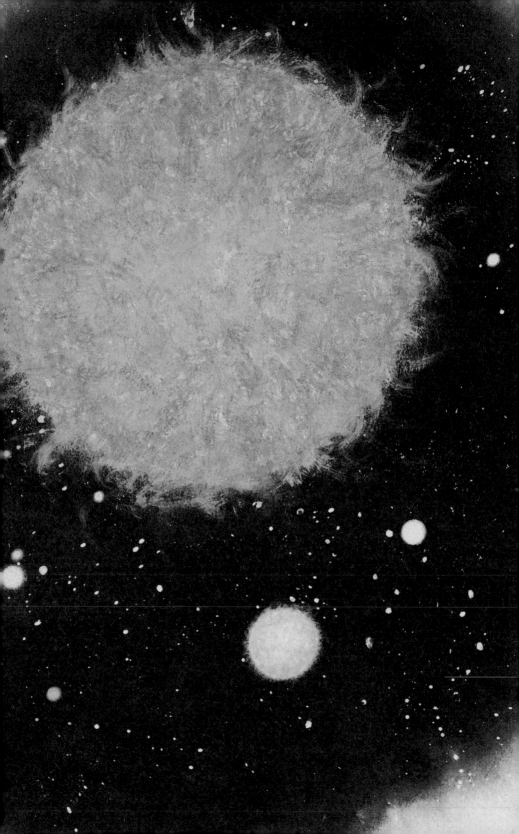

Light travels at a speed of 186,000 miles per second. A light year is the distance light travels in one year. That's a long way! We measure the distance from stars to our planet in light years because in miles the distance is too great to understand.

There is a very bright star, called Rigel, that is about 900 light years from Earth. If you see Rigel in the sky tonight, you are seeing the light that left that star around 900 years ago.

Rigel looks blue-white in the night sky. This tells scientists that Rigel is a very hot star. The color of a star tells us its temperature. In this way, a star is like a ball of very hot metal.

When the metal ball glows red, it is hot—but not as hot as it can be. When it glows yellow, it is hotter than when it was red. When it glows white, it is still hotter. And when it is blue-white, or blue, it is hottest of all.

We know that Rigel is extremely hot because its light is blue-white. Our own sun is a yellow star, so it is not as hot as Rigel.

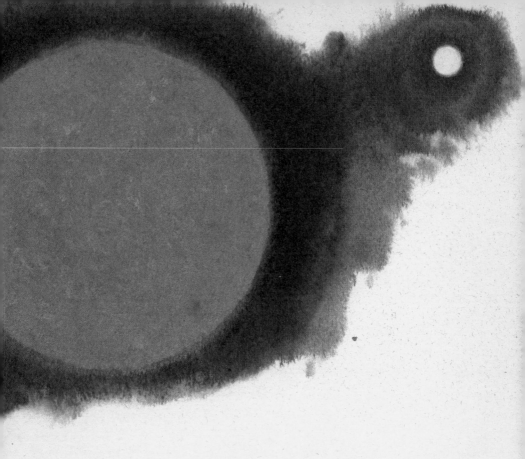

Another way of measuring stars is by their brightness, or magnitude. Our sun appears to be the brightest star. But the sun only seems so bright because it is so close to us.

Rigel is one of the brightest stars. Compared to a very bright star like Rigel, our sun is quite weak and dim.

All stars give off light and heat and other forms of energy. These are the result of nuclear reactions.

A star is made up mostly of two gases—hydrogen and helium. At the center of every atom of hydrogen or helium is something called a nucleus. When the nucleus of one hydrogen atom combines, or fuses, with the nucleus of another hydrogen atom, it is called *nuclear fusion.*

Two things happen at once. The hydrogen is changed into helium, and huge amounts of energy are released, in the form of light and heat and atomic radiation. That's how a star releases energy.

A hydrogen bomb also releases energy by nuclear fusion. But as powerful as it is, a hydrogen bomb is like the flicker of a firefly compared to the energy released by a star. As long as a star has hydrogen to use as nuclear fuel, it will continue to shine and send out light.

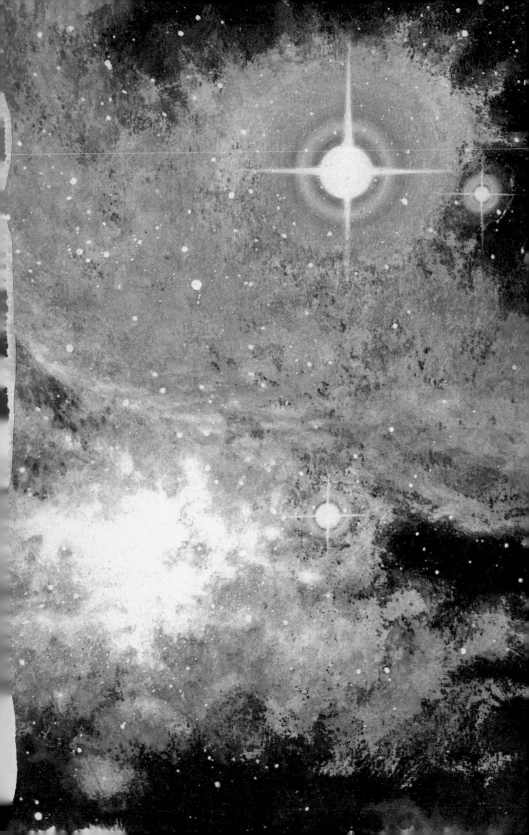

Starlight doesn't really twinkle. It just looks that way to us on Earth. Starlight is really a steady glow until it reaches the atmosphere around our planet.

As starlight passes through the atmosphere, it shifts and bounces and seems to be unsteady. When we see this unsteady light, we say the stars are twinkling.

When you gaze at the twinkling stars,
they all seem to be little dots of light. But if
you look through a powerful telescope, you
can see that there are many different kinds of
stars. Some are actually two stars very close
together—or even three or more stars.

Sometimes a star becomes much, much brighter for days, weeks, or months. Scientists call this kind of star a nova. *Nova* is a Latin word that means "new."

At other times a star becomes millions of times brighter, like a match flaring to life in a dark room. Then it fades away or seems to explode in a cloud of light. This kind of star is called a supernova.

After many years of studying novas and supernovas, scientists believe they know how stars form, how stars change, and how stars die. Stars are formed, they tell us, from huge clouds of gas and dust.

The gas and dust particles whirl around and around like a pinwheel. As they whirl, they are drawn together into a vast ball of gas. The particles on the outside press on the particles deep inside the ball of gas. The pressure gets so great and the ball gets so hot that the gases begin to glow. Finally, the pressure and the heat start a nuclear reaction. Now the gases have become a star.

It takes many millions of years for clouds of gas to become a star. And it may take billions of years for the hydrogen in a star to be used up.

Eventually, a star may expand and become a red giant, then shrink and turn into a white dwarf. Or a star may explode as a supernova, then become a neutron star. Or a star may expand and then collapse into a black hole, whose gravity is so strong that nothing can escape from it.

There are many clouds of gas and dust in space. Such a cloud is called a *nebula*, which is the Latin word for "mist." We can even see some nebulae without a telescope. The ones we see are the closest nebulae. They are part of our own galaxy.

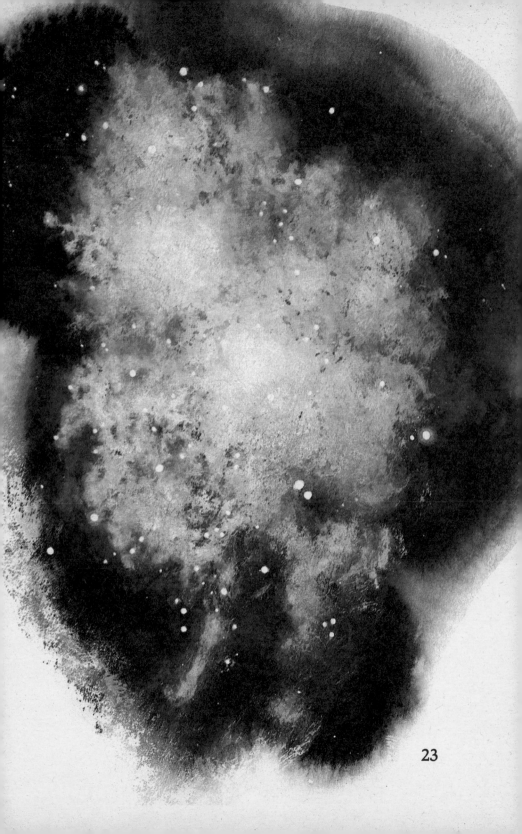

A galaxy is an enormous collection of millions and millions of stars. Our galaxy is called the Milky Way, because it looks like a splash of milk across the night sky. It is said to be a spiral galaxy, because it is shaped something like a pinwheel.

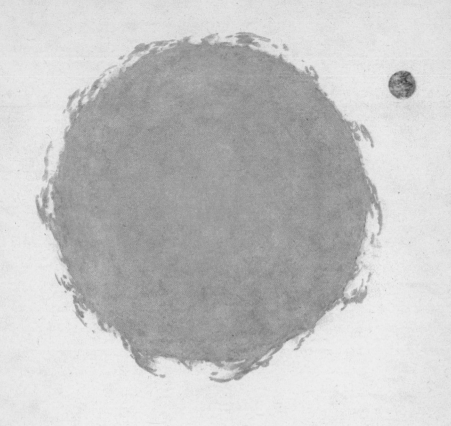

The Milky Way has more stars than anyone could count. They all travel around the center of the spiral. Our sun is one of those stars. It takes the sun about 200 million years to travel once around our galaxy.

There are billions of other galaxies in space. Some are spiral shaped, some are round, and some have no particular shape. Some of these galaxies are so far away that we are just beginning to learn about them.

Scientists use many tools in their study of the stars. There are giant telescopes with eyes that see deep into space and cameras that record what these eyes see.

There are instruments that pick up the sound waves and measure the radiation that come to us from distant stars and galaxies. And there are spacecraft sent up from Earth far above the atmosphere. All of these tools and machines are providing us with a rich store of information about the stars.

Before the twentieth century, most of these tools did not exist. But people have always been interested in the stars.

Thousands of years ago, when there were no clocks, people told time by looking at the night sky. They did this by picking out a group of stars that seemed to make a picture. They called these star groups constellations.

One of these constellations was named Orion, the hunter. You can see Orion on any clear night. He has two very bright stars for his shoulders. A row of three stars are his belt. Two more bright stars are his feet.

In the early evening, Orion is in the eastern part of the sky. As the night goes on, this constellation moves to the west. Orion's position in the sky tells us whether it is early evening, the middle of the night, or near dawn.

Long ago, people learned how to find their way at night by using one special star. It is sometimes called Polaris, the pole star. When you look at Polaris, you are facing north. So it is also known as the North Star.

Other stars and constellations move through the sky, but Polaris never changes its place. Polaris is always north. That is why, long before there were compasses, people used the North Star to guide them on trips across land or sea.

As the centuries went on, people invented instruments to help them use the stars. One of these instruments is the sextant. A sextant measures the exact angle between a star and the horizon. Using this information and maps of Earth, a ship's navigator can tell exactly where the ship is.

The stars have always been dependable guides to travelers on our planet. They have also been a source of wonder and beauty to people everywhere. And today, as we venture into space, the stars have become something more. They are a goal, a goal we may reach someday in the future.